THE WITCHES GO ON VACATION

Hatti

Grimly

Abbiewail

Scarea

Dedicated
to
Sophie

THE WITCHES GO ON VACATION

'Oh no,' sighed Postman Peter. 'Not another letter for Witchwood Manor.'

The one thing he didn't like to do was to deliver mail there! Any time he had to drop by with a parcel or a letter he always ended up the victim of one of those crazy witches' practical jokes. He checked his watch. It was very early. Perhaps they were all still in bed – he certainly hoped so.

He cycled as fast as he could up the tree-lined avenue. Meaty, the griffon vulture, squawked loudly as he spied the postman whizzing up the driveway.

'Quiet!' snapped Scarea as she turned over in her bed. 'I'm trying to catch up on my beauty sleep.'

Grimly was still snoring soundly in her room. Hatti blinked awake and yawned. Abbiewail had seen Postman Peter heading up the avenue so she was sneaking down the stairs with her wand at the ready.

Postman Peter's bike screeched to a halt at the front door. Nervously he looked around for any signs of ambush, but all seemed quiet. He gave a big sigh of relief.

The last time he had delivered a letter here, Abbiewail spotted him and did her magic on him. He hadn't realised until he went back to the post office and everyone began to laugh loudly at him. He didn't know why until he sat down and discovered he had grown a donkey's tail. It was very embarrassing. Every time a housefly appeared the tail would swish at it. His tail didn't disappear until the following day.

Today, thankfully, the coast seemed

clear. Postman Peter pushed up the letterbox flap to slide in the letter. Two eyes stared back at him. He gave out a loud shriek as the letter was yanked from his hand. As quick as a flash he turned his bike around and peddled furiously down the avenue.

'Ready, aim, fire!' grinned Abbiewail, as she aimed her wand out the letterbox.

A bolt of light shot from her wand and flew straight at the poor postman.

Postman Peter began to sense something was not right. His bike started to vanish in front of his eyes only to be replaced by a large frog. Abbiewail cackled loudly as she watched him hold on tightly as the bullfrog hopped down the avenue.

'That was fun,' said Abbiewail, as she wiped the tears of laughter from her eyes. 'I am wicked.'

She fingered Chompy, the tarantula, who was holding the letter between his fangs. Looking down, she was surprised to see that the letter was addressed to her.

'It's for me!' she shrieked with joy. 'How curious,' she said to herself then, for she rarely got mail.

The tarantula jumped out of her hand and scurried across the room with the letter.

'Oh, do stop fooling about,' snapped

Abbiewail, as Chompy hid under a chair. She reached under the chair, but the tarantula had scurried into the sitting room.

'Come back with my letter at once or I'll turn you into a moth. Now you wouldn't like that, would you?' she growled menacingly as she sneaked on all fours after the spider.

She pushed her hand quickly under the sofa, but Chompy was gone scurrying under the grandfather clock.

'Oh, you make me so mad at times,' squealed Abbiewail, shaking her body. Then pulling up her sleeves she pointed her wand at the clock.

'I'm counting up to three. If that letter is not in my hands by then you will be like a moth to a flame! I hope you understand my meaning?'

But the tarantula did not appear.

'One! Two!'

Just as Abbiewail was about to take aim with her wand, the letter was pushed out onto the carpet.

'About time,' she exclaimed, opening the envelope.

'What's all the noise about?' grumbled Grimly, when she heard loud shrieks and cackles coming from downstairs.

'GRIMLY! SCAREA! HATTI! Come quickly!' Abbiewail yelled loudly.

Hatti hopped onto her broom and shot out of her bedroom, crashing into Grimly and lifting her into the air.

'Aaahh!' yelled Grimly.

Abbiewail was running up the stairs,

12

waving the letter in the air, when she crashed straight into Grimly and Hatti. They tumbled down the stairs and landed in a heap on top of each other.

'Didn't I tell you before, Hatti, to walk down the stairs and not to use your broom?' snapped Grimly.

'Will you please remove your large frame from my person?' growled Abbiewail.

Scarea walked gracefully down the stairs with her pet vulture on her shoulder.

'Stop fooling about. You all look ridiculous,' she said crossly.

'So would you,' snapped Grimly, 'if you had been unceremoniously sent flying down the stairs.'

'That's what the banister is for, to prevent one from falling,' said Scarea.

'Will you all just be quiet for a minute?' demanded Abbiewail, as she settled herself. Then a broad grin broke across her face as she waved the letter at them.

'But I can't read without my glasses,' said Grimly.

'No,' said Abbiewail, 'you don't have to read it. I'm about to tell you all!'

'Couldn't you tell us at breakfast? Now that I'm awake I feel hungry,' said Scarea.

'So do I,' said Meaty, who was always hungry.

'But it's very important and exciting,' insisted Abbiewail. Then her expression changed.

'What is it?' asked Grimly. 'You have that look of the cat who just ate the pet canary.'

'She tried to turn me into a moth just because I was having a little fun,' sighed the tarantula, as he crawled up on Grimly's shoulder.

'Ah, you poor thing,' said Grimly, stroking Chompy's head. 'Was Auntie Abbiewail teasing and scaring you?'

The spider nodded up and down.

'I was trying to tell you something good about this letter,' said Abbiewail. 'Then I remembered something I did that was a little naughty . . . '

'Good and bad news,' said Scarea. 'How

15

delightful! We'll have to hear it over breakfast.'

'But I want to tell you all now.' Abbiewail jumped up and down.

'No need for tantrums,' said Grimly. 'Not in front of our dear niece.'

'I don't mind,' said Hatti. 'It's funny to look at.'

'Will you all be quiet!' yelled Fangy, the vampire bat, from the red velvet curtains. 'Can't a guy get some sleep around here, after all I'm trying to hibernate?'

'Don't be silly,' scolded Scarea. 'Bats don't hibernate in summer.'

'Oops, you're right,' said Fangy. 'I must have been dreaming it was wintertime. Yes, I remember . . . snow was falling, it was night-time, I was all snuggled up on the curtains and there was a warm fire blazing . . . '

'Will you be quiet,' snapped Abbiewail. 'I have something much more important to announce.'

'Suit yourself. If you don't want to hear about my dream that's fine, I'm not upset,' sighed the bat.

'You are all so annoying . . . ' said Abbiewail. She looked around but the others had gone into the kitchen and were tucking into breakfast.

'Now, sister dear,' Grimly smiled. 'Tell us about the contents of the letter.'

'First the bad news,' Scarea retorted. 'We might as well start the morning off well.'

'Well, this morning when Nosy Parker Postman Peter arrived with this letter for me . . . ' Abbiewail began.

'Why do you call him Nosy Parker?' enquired Hatti.

'Well, because when he does bring us a delivery, and especially if it's a parcel, he's dying to know what's inside,' said Scarea.

'I am trying to tell you what happened earlier,' snapped Abbiewail.

'We're all ears,' said Grimly.

'Well, I decided to have a bit of fun with Postman Peter,' she continued. 'I couldn't resist taking out my wand and turning him into a large frog, but I missed with my shot and turned his bike into a frog instead,' she chuckled. 'It was even funnier, actually, to watch him try and stay on the frog as it hopped down the avenue.' She laughed again. 'It was like something you'd see in one of those rodeo shows where the cowboy is trying to stay on a bull. It was a hoot!' She grinned broadly. 'Only now I feel guilty since he brought me this special letter.'

'How long will the spell last?' asked Scarea.

'About twenty-four hours, I think,' replied Abbiewail.

'We must cancel the spell right away,' said Grimly. 'Hatti, would you be a pet and fly after the postman and break the spell so the poor fellow can go back to the village with his proper transport?'

'Right away, Aunt Grimly,' said Hatti, bolting down her cereal and gulping her orange juice.

'Now before you go . . . ' said Grimly, 'let me think, what is the magic for turning a frog back into a bicycle? Is it *Do be, do be, do*?'

'That sounds like a song,' Scarea quipped.

'Oh yes, you're right.' Grimly giggled. 'Silly me. Now it must be . . . '

'It's okay, Aunt Grimly. I know the words.' Hatti quickly leaped onto her broom and was gone like a flash through the open kitchen window.

'I wish that child would use the door like any normal person,' said Grimly.

'None of you are normal,' Meaty sniggered.

They all stared at the vulture. He swallowed hard.

'What I mean is . . . who wants to be normal?'

'He's quite right,' laughed Grimly.

'Now, can I please tell you the contents of my letter?' grumbled Abbiewail.

'We should really wait until Hatti gets back so she can get the news first hand,' suggested Meaty.

'You're all impossible,' snapped Abbiewail, as she poured another bowl of cereal for herself. What she didn't realise was that Chompy had crawled into her bowl. She poured in the milk and sprinkled some sugar over him. The spider was happily lapping up the sweet milk and nibbling the cereal when a spoon went into the bowl and scooped him up. Abbiewail rammed the spoon into her mouth, not realising she had just taken the spider into her mouth also.

'Yuck!' she exclaimed as she spat Chompy out. 'I think that cereal is stale.'

The spider went shooting across the room and crashed into the wall. He slid down and, feeling very dizzy, he staggered into a mousehole.

'Your table manners have gone to the dogs,' snapped Scarea.

'Just as well Mammah is not here,' said Grimly. 'She was a stickler for good table manners.'

Hatti searched all around for Postman Peter. He wasn't anywhere to be seen. She tried for him along the road to Gigglebrook village, but the only thing on the road was an old crow picking up some grit to help him with his digestion.

'Excuse me, Mr Crow, I was wondering did you see Postman Peter.'

'See him?' said the crow. 'He nearly scared the wits out of me, leaping about on a thing that looked like a giant frog. Why can't he stick with his bike or a car? At least then I could hear him coming.'

'Where did he go?' enquired Hatti.

'He just leaped over that hedgerow over there,' replied the crow, pointing with his wing away over the fields.

'Thanks, Mr Crow,' shouted Hatti as she flew over the hedge and across the fields.

Up ahead she could see a flock of sheep scattering in all directions. She knew the postman must be there.

'Help!' yelled Postman Peter, trying to stay on the hopping mad frog.

The sheep just answered: 'Baah!'

Now the frog was heading for a large lake.

'Oh no!' shrieked the postman, as they got nearer to the water.

Hatti pulled out her wand, took careful aim, said the magic words and fired her magic from her wand.

'Bullseye!' she cheered as it hit the frog.

There was a flash of colourful light and

Postman Peter was back on his bike trying to steer it. But the bike hit the stump of a tree, overturned and sent Postman Peter flying into the air and splashing into the centre of the lake.

Hatti thought she had better make herself scarce in case Postman Peter thought she had done that to him on purpose. She sped away, looking over her shoulder once to see a very wet postman crawling out of the lake.

'What's keeping that child?' grumbled Abbiewail. 'I've been waiting all morning to tell you my good news.'

'She's only been gone a few minutes,' said Scarea.

The hall door suddenly swung open and Hatti flew in on her broom. As she reached the kitchen she jumped off on to a chair and watched the broom park itself in the broom cupboard.

'Mission accomplished,' said Hatti proudly.

'At last,' said Abbiewail. 'Now, are you ready to hear my good news?'

'We can't wait,' said Hatti.

Abbiewail began to read the letter.

Dear Ms Abbiewail Grimalot,

We are pleased to inform you that you have won our first prize of a family holiday tour of the European capital cities.

'Wow!' said Hatti.

'Bravo!' said Scarea, clapping her hands.

'How very exciting,' remarked Grimly, adding: 'How did you win such a wonderful holiday, Abbie dear?'

'Oh, I just cleverly answered a few questions for a competition which was on the back of my favourite cereal box.'

Grimly looked suspicious. 'Are you sure you didn't use your magic to get the answers?'

'That's typical, accusing me in the wrong.'

'My dear, you are not exactly known for your brain power,' quipped Scarea.

'That's perfectly charming,' snapped

Abbiewail. 'I've a good mind to go on my own after those hurtful remarks.'

'We didn't mean to hurt you, dear. We were only kidding,' said Scarea.

'It's wonderful about the prize, it's only a pity you didn't tell us sooner,' smiled Grimly.

'Oooooh, I could scream,' declared Abbiewail. 'But I won't, I'll zip my lips!'

As the day approached for their holiday the witches could hardly contain their excitement. Scarea danced around the house and sang brightly. Hatti was the first packed and was preparing breakfast. Grimly was fussing about what to wear and how much she should bring on holidays. Abbiewail had been phoning around telling all her friends about her win. She asked Count Dracula could he please mind Fangy while they were away. But he declined, saying he was suffering from an allergy to bats. He hoped it would clear up soon as it was very embarrassing.

'Never mind,' said Scarea, 'we'll bring them all – Fangy, Chompy and Meaty.'

When they were all packed, Grimly announced that they should leave their wands and their broomsticks behind. None of the others seemed too pleased with the idea, but they said nothing.

'We'll bring our hats of course,' said Grimly. 'I'd feel almost naked without mine.'

'I think we should look a bit more colourful when we are travelling to all those exciting cities,' said Scarea.

They all produced their wands and changed their black clothes into something more bright and cheerful. Hatti changed her clothes for jeans and a T-shirt.

'It will take some time to get used to all this cheerfulness,' chuckled Abbiewail.

'Would it not be easier to fly on our brooms to the airport?' suggested Scarea.

'No! We'll use Pappah's old car, it could do with a spin,' said Grimly.

Abbiewail bent over and whispered into Hatti's ear. 'Thank you for not telling them that you answered nearly all of the questions for the competition.'

'It's our secret,' smiled Hatti.

'I will buy you a big ice cream in Rome when we get there,' winked Abbiewail.

'This is the final call for passengers!' announced the stewardess over the loudspeaker in the departure lounge.

'We're here!' shrieked Grimly, as she ran up waving her boarding pass in the air, followed by Scarea, Hatti and Abbiewail, who was puffing and panting.

'This is so exciting,' said Hatti as they became airborne.

Abbiewail had her eyes tightly shut and was trembling all over.

'What's the matter?' asked Hatti.

'Oh, it's just that it's my first time flying and I'm terrified,' whimpered Abbiewail.

'Don't be ridiculous,' scolded Scarea. 'You fly every day on your broom.'

Abbiewail opened her eyes and smiled broadly. 'You're quite right, dear sister. I have flown before, many's the time. Thank you for reminding me.'

Hatti laughed loudly at her silly aunt. Then the stewardess came around with trays of food. Scarea looked aghast.

'Plastic cups! We're used to china and silver.'

'I'm used to bigger helpings than this,' Abbiewail grumbled.

'I'd love some of my favourite marmalade,' sighed Grimly.

Hatti thought for a moment and decided

there was a way of pleasing them all. She produced her wand and in a twinkle there was silver cutlery and pure white china along with all their favourite breakfasts.

'How delightful!' said Scarea.

'This is wonderful!' chuckled Grimly. Then she said to Hatti: 'I thought we had agreed no wands.'

Hatti looked embarrassed. 'Well, I brought mine in case of an emergency.'

'Leave the child alone,' said Scarea. 'And enjoy your breakfast.'

'What about us?' asked the vulture. 'I know you made us invisible so that we could sneak aboard the plane, but we're getting very hungry watching all that food being served.'

'Don't worry,' said Hatti. Using her wand again she made some lovely invisible food for the vulture, the spider and the bat.

'Well, this is the first time we've had invisible food,' said Meaty. 'And if I do say so, it tastes delicious.'

The first stop on their holiday in Europe was Amsterdam.

'Oh, this is so exciting,' said Grimly. 'We are actually in Holland.'

'They say there are over 1000 bridges in Amsterdam,' said Hatti.

'My, you are full of information,' said Abbiewail. 'Maybe sending you to school wasn't a bad idea after all.'

Grimly pulled out her wand. 'I think we should wear clogs now that we're here.'

'I thought you insisted on not bringing your wand,' said Scarea.

'Oh, did I?' grinned Grimly. 'In all the excitement I must have forgotten.' She aimed at Abbiewail's boots and turned them into clogs. Then she did the same to her own and the others. Hatti found that her clogs took a bit of getting used to when walking, but she managed better than Grimly and Abbiewail.

Then Grimly turned the footwear of everyone who passed by into clogs. Hatti found it very funny, but the people walking by didn't seem to think so, as they had no idea how it had happened.

In the afternoon they sat outside a restaurant near one of the many canals.

'I was expecting more windmills,' said Scarea.

'I thought there would be more swans on the canals,' added Grimly.

'I think there should be more tulips in the city,' suggested Abbiewail.

'Well, I think it's beautiful,' said Hatti.

'There's always room for improvement,' insisted Scarea, pulling out her wand from her bag.

'I thought we were going to leave our wands at home,' snapped Abbiewail.

'Well, if dear Grimly and darling Hatti could bring theirs I don't see why I shouldn't have brought mine,' retorted Scarea.

'Well, in that case it's only fair I should have brought mine too,' said Abbiewail, pulling hers from inside her sleeve. They all laughed loudly.

Grimly took aim at the water, said some magic and in an instant there were swans everywhere, packed like sardines all along the canal, flapping their wings and hissing.

'Charming isn't it,' beamed Grimly.

'I want more tulips,' declared Abbiewail, waving her wand all about.

But nothing happened.

'What's wrong with this stupid wand?' grumbled Abbiewail. 'I hope all the travelling hasn't affected it.'

'You forgot to say the magic words, dear,' said Scarea.

'Oh, of course,' chuckled Abbiewail. 'Silly me.' She said the magic words and Bingo! There were tulips everywhere –

some growing on roofs, in trees, out through chimneys, even on ladies' sun hats!

'What a beautiful spread of colour,' said Abbiewail proudly.

'My turn,' giggled Scarea. With an impish grin she said her magic words and aimed her wand at different parts of the city. Suddenly windmills began to mushroom up everywhere there was an empty space – in car parks, in people's back gardens, in parks.

'I hope I haven't overdone it,' she said to herself as the windmills began to spin, causing a strong wind to blow. Newspapers and hats were sent flying into the air and flower-pots crashed to the ground.

'It's getting a little windy around here. I think it's time to go,' suggested Scarea.

That evening when things were quiet and the rest of the family had gone to bed,

Hatti flew out through her bedroom window and over the city to try and put things back to normal. She zapped all the extra swans first, making them vanish. The two resident swans were very grateful as the canal was getting rather overcrowded. The tulips were next to be removed. There were plenty to see in the flower shops and parks without Abbiewail's additions.

As Hatti whizzed over the city, a policeman, who was on the beat near the canal, got such a shock that he accidentally stepped backwards into the water. The swans hissed and flapped at him. He swam as quickly as he could to the far side of the canal and crawled out. He looked a very sorry sight as he squelched back to the police station.

The swans finally had the canal to themselves, and were proud of the way they had chased off the human intruder. It was bad enough having all those extra swans around all afternoon, but for humans to start getting in on the act – it was too much.

Hatti felt a bit sorry for the policeman. She shot a bolt of magic at him, hoping it would dry him off. The only problem was that the words she used made his uniform vanish and she couldn't remember the words to bring it back. She hoped he had a spare uniform in the station, as she watched him run down the road in his 'birthday suit'.

Hatti gave a big yawn. It was tiring work, performing all this magic. And there were still the windmills to be removed. She quickly flew about, vanished them all in one swish of her wand, then hurried home.

'Time to get up,' said Abbiewail to a bleary-eyed Hatti. 'You can't stay in bed all morning. We are heading for gay Paris. Isn't it exciting, taking the train to France?'

Sitting in their first-class carriage, Hatti couldn't help noticing the newspaper a gentleman was reading. The headline read, *'Windmills Vanish From Amsterdam'*.

Scarea read it too.

'Well, that's ridiculous!' she exclaimed. 'You know, dear sisters, how I made extra ones. It just goes to show, you can't believe a word that they write in the newspapers.'

Hatti began to wonder had she vanished

more windmills than she should have.

Abbiewail pointed her wand at the newspaper and it shot out of the man's hand and flew over to her. She scanned it quickly.

'No mention of the swans or tulips, only windmills!' she grumbled.

The man got up from his seat, went over to Abbiewail and demanded his paper back. Snatching it from her hands he returned to his seat.

'The cheek!' he muttered to himself.

Abbiewail aimed her wand at the paper and turned it into a comic. The man couldn't believe his eyes. Businessmen passing up along the carriage looked disapprovingly at the man. One man commented to another as they headed for breakfast: 'Some people never grow up.'

The smell of food wafting down the carriage was irresistible.

'Let's have breakfast,' suggested Grimly.

'Good idea, sister dear,' they agreed, and wandered off to the dining carriage.

They all ate a hearty breakfast. Since Fangy, Meaty and Chompy were still invisible they had great fun eating all the other people's breakfasts without their knowing. The people kept ordering second breakfasts after accusing the waiter of only bringing empty plates. The poor waiter didn't know what was happening.

When they arrived in Paris, Scarea insisted that the first place they should visit was the Louvre.

'It's okay, I went earlier,' said Grimly.

'Not the loo!' snapped Scarea. 'The Louvre – one of the finest art galleries in the world.'

'I knew that,' said Hatti. 'It's where the Mona Lisa is.'

'I didn't know she was living in Paris,' said Abbiewail.

'Oh, I give up,' sighed Scarea. 'When it comes to the arts, dear sisters, I fear your education is sadly lacking. We're talking about the famous painting.'

'Oh, don't be such a snob,' retorted Abbiewail. 'I don't see why this Mona Lisa couldn't have her photograph taken like everyone else.'

Hatti laughed loudly at this. Abbiewail didn't know why.

That first morning in Paris they went to the famous Louvre gallery. Hatti was delighted to see all the lovely paintings. A book in her school library showed some of these famous paintings, but they were only prints. Here she was standing in front of the originals. It was amazing!

'There it is,' said Abbiewail.

'Yes, dear sister,' said Scarea. 'La Gioconda. Look at her wonderful mysterious smile.'

'Call that a smile,' retorted Abbiewail. 'I've seen better smiles on a fish.'

'You're a philistine, Abbiewail.'

'How dare you call me a philis-time.'

'Calm down,' chuckled Grimly.

'Well, I don't think she should call me something until I look it up in the dictionary,' Abbiewail complained.

Nearby a guide was speaking to a large group of tourists: 'It is said that Leonardo engaged musicians to play and sing, and jesters to keep her merry . . . '

'They didn't do a very good job,' said Abbiewail.

'Let's go and have lunch,' suggested Grimly. 'Looking at all these paintings makes one exhausted and very hungry.'

Scarea sighed. 'Well, at least my

appreciation of the arts and the finer things in life have passed on to *you*, dear niece.'

'Oh yes,' said Hatti, a little puzzled by the remark.

As they left the museum Abbiewail pretended to drop her handkerchief. She sneaked back to the Mona Lisa painting, aimed her wand and with a few magic words shot a bolt of light at the painting.

'That's better,' grinned Abbiewail, hurrying out of the museum.

A short time later, the curator's jaw dropped when he passed by the painting. The Mona Lisa had the biggest smile he had ever seen, as well as a witch's hat on her head!

Later in the afternoon they travelled by cruise boat up the River Seine to visit the Eiffel Tower. After that Hatti brought Fangy, Chompy and Meaty up to the top of Notre Dame de Paris to get an aerial view of the city. She didn't fancy going up all the steps so she flew up to the top on her broom, racing the vulture to see who reached there first. By the time she arrived at the top Meaty was sitting up beside a gargoyle, stretching his wings and grinning to himself. A group of American tourists passed by, carrying cameras and eating hot dogs. As they stopped to take a picture of

Meaty, thinking he was a statue, he snatched the hot dogs from their hands, sending them hurrying in a panic for the exit.

'What a beautiful view,' said Hatti as she alighted on top of a gargoyle. She was surprised how few visitors there were. Meaty just sniggered.

'You smell of hot dogs,' said Chompy to Meaty.

'Did you ever smell your own breath?' snapped the vulture.

'Please, let's not be snapping at each other,' said Hatti. 'Enjoy the lovely view.'

'Look,' said Fangy. 'The Eiffel Tower is upside down.'

'It's you who's upside down,' said Chompy.

'Oh, you're right,' grinned the vampire bat, adjusting his position. 'I never realised the Eiffel Tower was pink in colour.'

'What!' said Hatti, taking her eye from the Sacré Coeur cathedral to where the Eiffel Tower was. Sure enough it was a bright pink. She knew it must be the work of one of her mischievous aunts.

Later that evening, when they were all having dinner together, Hatti mentioned that she saw the Eiffel Tower from Notre Dame and that it had changed colour to a bright pink.

'Well, don't look at me,' said Abbiewail. 'I only changed the Mona Lisa's thin little smile to a broad grin.'

'You did what?' said Scarea. 'How could you do that to La Gioconda?'

'Well, I was only trying to improve on it a little.'

'How can you improve on perfection?' scolded Scarea.

'Listen to you talking! What about you

putting new arms on the Venus de Milo?'

'Well, she did have them once,' retorted Scarea.

'I'm the guilty one!' Grimly piped up. 'I just thought a pink tower would be in keeping with this beautiful city.'

'I agree,' said Abbiewail. 'Although I would have preferred a bright yellow colour myself.'

Hatti didn't think the Parisians would be too pleased with the various changes in their city. So when her aunts finally went to bed in the evening, she jumped on her broom and headed first to the Eiffel Tower

and returned it to its original metal colour. The tower looked magical all lit up.

Her next task was to get past the security guards in the Louvre and return the painting of the Mona Lisa to its former glory. Hatti shot a bolt from her wand at one of the windows and it opened, sending the alarms off all over the building. The security men began to panic and ran into each other, spilling their coffee and dropping their baguettes. 'What is happening?' they wondered, checking all the television monitors.

The sound of police cars could be heard as they drove at speed to the Louvre. Hatti flew inside the gallery; flying in and out of different rooms trying to remember which room the masterpiece was in. Finally she found the painting. She aimed her wand and magicked the Mona Lisa back to its original form.

One of the security men could not believe his eyes when he looked in his monitor and saw what looked like a young girl, dressed like a witch, flying about on a broom. Next minute, hundreds of French police hurried into the museum, running up and down the different stairs and checking every room. In all the confusion Hatti flew out over their heads and escaped out the same window she had entered, but not before she undid Scarea's magic on the Venus de Milo.

By the time Hatti got back to her hotel room she was exhausted. But at least the painting and the sculpture were returned to normal and the famous Eiffel Tower was its proper colour again.

'Rise and shine,' said Grimly, shaking Hatti awake. 'We're on the move again.'

Hatti rubbed the tiredness from her eyes.

'Where to this time?' she yawned.

'The Eternal City,' said Scarea, who was passing by her room.

'Oh, she means Rome, dear,' chuckled Grimly.

After breakfast they were on a coach to Italy. On the way, Scarea decided to improve her tan. She changed into her swimming togs and stretched out above the roof.

'Show off!' grumbled Abbiewail, as she watched her sister flying overhead.

When eventually they reached Rome they decided to visit the Colosseum.

'Oh, isn't this splendid,' said Grimly. 'I can just see Charlton Heston on his chariot rushing over to rescue me!'

'No! It would be the real Mark Antony,' said Scarea, 'rescuing me. And I, of course, would be Cleopatra.'

'Who would I be?' asked Abbiewail.

'You could be one of those serving girls throwing flowers on the path as we walked by.'

'I don't want to be a serving girl, I want to be Julius Caesar's wife – only I'm the boss.'

'Oh, let's do it. It would be fun,' grinned Grimly.

Hatti began to regret that they had brought their wands. 'Couldn't we just enjoy the sights, soak up the atmosphere, buy some ice cream?' pleaded Hatti.

'Oh, don't be an old stick-in-the-mud,' said Abbiewail, as she pulled up her sleeves and took aim at the ancient building.

Zapping the Colosseum with her magic, she made it look as it was two thousand years ago. Then she aimed at the busy traffic of cars, buses and lorries whizzing by. Whispering her magic words, a wall of light appeared across the road. As the traffic went through it the cars and buses were immediately transformed into chariots and wagons. Lorries became carts, and bikes were turned into horses or donkeys. The car owners looked in disbelief as they drove around in their new chariots.

'They do look rather ridiculous in modern clothes,' said Scarea. 'I don't think I'm quite finished yet,' she chuckled, as she turned people's suits into togas, their jackets into cloaks and their hats into ancient Roman helmets.

'Now, it's my turn,' she added, changing herself into Cleopatra. 'And finally, to conjure up handsome Mark Antony . . . ' She made her magic and closed her eyes.

But Abbiewail said some magic words too and waved her wand at the same time.

'Kiss me, Mark Antony, I am Queen of the Nile,' announced Scarea.

'I don't kiss girls,' said a small voice.

Scarea opened her eyes to see an eight-year-old boy. 'You're Mark Antony?'

The boy nodded.

'But something is wrong here. You're supposed to be an adult on a golden chariot.'

Abbiewail couldn't keep in her laughter.

'It was you!' snapped Scarea, as she aimed her wand at her sister. 'You turned him into a little boy.'

'Temper! Temper!' said Abbiewail. 'You try any magic on me and I'll give you back as good as I get.'

'You know I am the best at magic around here,' said Scarea in menacing tones.

'Oh, is that so?' said Abbiewail. 'Well, let me tell you, I know all about your secret magic books because I've read them all!' She cackled loudly.

'Sisters, please. We're on holidays. Let's not start arguing,' pleaded Grimly.

'Well, she started it,' snapped Abbiewail.

'No, I didn't,' said Scarea. 'This sister of mine is trying to ruin my great moment in history.'

'You'll be history if you keep this up,' growled Abbiewail.

'What kind of talk is that, sister?' scolded Grimly. 'It sounds like something straight out of those American police series on TV.'

Hatti decided to make herself scarce and invited the young Mark Antony for an ice cream in the ice cream parlour.

'Can we come?' asked Meaty.

'Yes, but you'll have to become invisible,' insisted Hatti.

'Sure,' said Meaty. 'We're getting used to it at this stage.'

Grimly was still trying to make peace between her sisters, while all around them chariots, wagons and carts whizzed by out of control. Abbiewail and Scarea were each hiding behind pillars shooting at each other with their wands.

'Missed!' shrieked Abbiewail, as a bolt of lightning bounced off the pillar she was hiding behind. Then Abbiewail took aim, turning her sister's chariot into an old cart.

'How dare you!' shrieked Scarea. 'I am the Queen of the Nile.'

'Enough of this,' thought Grimly. She raised her wand and said a few magical words. 'I know a thing or two about ancient history too.'

There were loud shrieks from the crowds as a herd of African elephants came charging down the road, trampling chariots and knocking down old wooden buildings.

'Aahh!' yelled Scarea, 'Where did they come from?'

'They're elephants,' declared Grimly, ducking for cover alongside Scarea and Abbiewail. The two sisters had forgotten their differences now that this new crisis had popped up.

'I know they're elephants,' snapped Scarea, 'but what are they doing here? They're ruining my show.'

'They belong to Hannibal . . . isn't he

divine sitting so proud up there on his elephant?' chuckled Grimly.

'But he comes much earlier in history,' moaned Scarea.

'Early or late . . . Aagh!' shrieked Abbiewail. 'Would you please tell this pachyderm to put me down?'

Scarea looked over at Hannibal. 'Would you be a dear and ask your cute elephant to put my sister down.'

'Your wish is my command,' replied Hannibal.

'So charming, and such good manners, even from those ancient days. Let's get things back to normal around here,' said Scarea. 'Fancy a cappuccino, my dear Hannibal?'

'I'm here to do battle,' said the soldier proudly.

'Oh, plenty of time for all that silly fighting,' said Grimly. 'I think sometimes you men never grow up.'

They joined Hatti who was eating an ice cream float with young Mark Antony. Up until now the owner of the parlour had been looking on very suspiciously at Hatti and her friend, but when he saw the others arrive, one dressed like an ancient soldier, he became very curious.

'Waiter! Four cappuccinos and four bakewell tarts with ice cream,' ordered Scarea. Smiling broadly at Hannibal she moved over to him.

'You're such a hunk,' she cooed.

'Excuse me, Signora, are you making a movie?' asked the owner.

'No,' snapped Abbiewail. 'This is the real thing, buster.'

Scarea looked at Hannibal with his cloak and armour.

'What you need is a nice Gucci suit.'

She waved her wand over him. In an instant he was completely transformed – suit, shirt, tie and sunglasses.

'That's better,' smiled Scarea.

'And just as handsome,' added Grimly.

Hannibal sat looking very confused, but enjoying his coffee.

'Meet Mark Antony,' said Hatti.

The young boy shook Hannibal's hand. 'I've heard the name,' he said.

'Let's not talk history,' grumbled Abbiewail. 'It's so boring. Tell me, dear Hannibal, are you married?'

'Don't be so nosy,' snapped Scarea.

'Ladies, please . . . we've got company,' said Grimly.

Hannibal looked down at his plate which was empty. He wondered how his dessert had vanished. Meaty chuckled and licked his lips.

'Well, I really must go,' said Hannibal. 'We march on Rome!' he bellowed.

'But you're here already,' said Scarea.

'No, I must cross the Alps and brave the elements on my African elephants,' he declared.

'I must go as well,' said Mark Antony. 'A soothsayer foretold that some day I too would be a famous soldier and that I would fall in love with a beautiful queen.'

'That was supposed to happen earlier,' Scarea complained. 'Something must have gone wrong with my magic.'

Abbiewail grinned but said nothing.

'Well, if you must, go,' said Scarea. 'We won't stand in the way of history.' She clicked her fingers and Hannibal vanished.

'How did you do that?' said Abbiewail.

'That's for me to know and you to find out,' Scarea retorted.

Mark Antony thanked Hatti for the ice cream and said he might bring the idea back to ancient Rome. Hatti smiled and shook his hand. Then she waved her wand over him and he was gone.

'Well, that was a very interesting experience,' said Grimly.

Suddenly Abbiewail started laughing uncontrollably.

'What is it?' snapped Scarea.

'You have just sent Hannibal back to his own time in a Gucci suit.'

'Well, he'll be the best dressed soldier on the battlefield,' sniggered Scarea.

Soon they were all laughing loudly at the idea of the great Carthaginian general, sitting on an African elephant in his designer suit, giving orders to his soldiers as they crossed the snowy Alps.

That evening at dinner on the Piazza Navona they were still laughing at the idea of Hannibal in a Gucci suit.

'We must pull ourselves together,' insisted Grimly, as she hooted with laughter. 'I know, maybe we should think of something sad. That would cure us.'

'We'll be going home soon,' said Scarea trying to think of something to say.

'What about Copenhagen, Stockholm, Berlin, Brussels, Lisbon, Madrid, Prague, Dublin, London, Geneva? I wonder did I leave any out?' murmured Abbiewail, counting the different European capitals on her fingers.

'You didn't expect they would send us to all those places,' said Scarea.

'You mustn't be greedy,' added Grimly. 'We've seen Amsterdam, Paris and Rome.'

'Well, I suppose it's a start,' said Abbiewail.

'I've really enjoyed myself,' said Hatti, a little relieved that they were going home soon. She loved visiting all the different places, but it was hard work dealing with her aunts wanting to make changes everywhere they went.

Early next morning Scarea entered Hatti's room. 'Still sleeping?'

'No,' yawned Hatti.

'Get dressed, child. We have a surprise trip planned.'

'Oh no!' sighed Hatti, sensing more trouble brewing.

As she entered the dining room for breakfast, her Aunt Grimly told her there was a bonus trip to Pisa. 'Isn't it exciting!'

'I personally would have preferred Florence or Venice,' said Scarea.

'There you go again, never pleased and to think that we're getting it all free.'

'Don't throw a wobbly,' said Scarea. 'I only . . .'

'What's this about a pizza?' said Abbiewail, rubbing her eyes as she entered the dining room. 'You know I like poached eggs on toast for breakfast. Why do we have to have pizza? Pizza's more suitable for lunch or dinner, not breakfast. Why does Scarea have to get her way all the time?'

'I haven't the faintest idea what you are talking about,' said Grimly.

'I was having a lovely dream when Scarea barged into my room and yelled "Get up! We're all going to eat pizza!"'

'If you took the cotton wool out of your ears, you would have heard me properly,' snapped Scarea. 'I walked into your room and informed you that we were all going to Pisa.'

'Oh,' said Abbiewail blankly.

'Yes, it's a bonus trip. The local travel agent informed me,' smiled Grimly.

'How come she didn't inform me? After all, I won the trip,' Abbiewail complained.

'Did somebody mention a pizza? I hope it's got meat on it,' said the vulture.

'You close that beak of yours,' said Abbiewail, 'or I'll turn you into a sparrow.'

'Who got out the wrong side of the bed then?' retorted Meaty.

'Are we going by coach or train?' asked Hatti.

'Train, I do believe,' said Grimly.

The trip to Pisa seemed to go without any hitch. They all enjoyed walking around the Leaning Tower of Pisa and getting their pictures taken. Hatti even bought a souvenir of the tower to bring home. No one used their wands or their brooms. In fact, they all acted just like ordinary tourists. Hatti was amazed but very pleased.

On the way back home in the plane the witches all agreed they'd had a wonderful time. Scarea thanked Abbiewail for being so clever at winning the competition.

'Oh, it was nothing,' grinned Abbiewail all pleased with herself.

They all cheered and sang *'For She's a Jolly Good Fellow . . .'*

'Home at last,' said Grimly as she kicked off her boots inside the hall door.

'It's wonderful to travel,' sighed Scarea. 'But it's nice to get home.'

Meaty hopped on his favourite perch and stretched his wings. Fangy and Chompy headed for the red velvet curtains and settled down for a good rest.

Hatti brought the travel bags up to the different rooms, then put away the wands.

'It's time for supper,' said Abbiewail. She hurried into the kitchen and made some toast and tea. 'Here, my dears,' she smiled, carrying in the tray of food and drinks.

They sat around having supper and resting.

'Let's see what's on television,' said Grimly. 'There might be some good old late night spooky film with Peter Cushing.'

' . . . And now, before our late night horror double bill,' said the announcer, 'we have a news flash. It appears that the famous Leaning Tower of Pisa has straightened itself. One eye witness said it was like magic . . . '

'How very strange,' said Scarea. 'We were there only yesterday and it was still leaning over.'

'No mention of the Mona Lisa, the windmills, or any other magic we performed,' mumbled Grimly, a little disappointed.

Abbiewail began to chuckle. Soon she was in hoots of laughter.

'What is it?' asked Scarea.

'Well . . . Hee, Hee. I have to admit it was me. I just couldn't resist straightening the Tower,' admitted Abbiewail.

'Isn't that typical! All the magic we performed and it's you who gets mentioned,' Scarea grumbled.

'Well, mine was obviously the best,' said Abbiewail. 'Why else would it be on television?'

'My magic is far superior,' snapped Scarea.

'Sisters please, the first movie – *The Raven* – is about to begin and it has the wonderful Vincent Price in it. Oh, goodie!'

'I think I'll get an early night,' said Hatti.

'Good idea, darling.'

Hatti kissed them all and headed out of the room. Only she wasn't going to her bedroom. First she had to undo her aunt's magic. Grabbing her broom, wand and cloak, she flew out through the landing window and eastwards across the starry sky. It was at times like this that she wished she could do magic at a distance.

It was the fastest she had ever travelled on a broom back to Italy and Pisa. She got there just as the television cameras were arriving to film the event. From the safety of a cathedral roof Hatti took aim at the Tower. In a flash it was back to its original position. She laughed loudly at the expressions on the reporters' faces when they realised the Tower was not straight any more.

It was early morning before Hatti got back home. She was very tired and found it exceedingly difficult not to fall asleep on her broom. Luckily the dawn chorus began and the beautiful bird songs made her stay awake. Finally she saw Witchwood Manor looming ahead. She picked up speed and hurried over the woods.

Below her, coming through a clearing, she saw Postman Peter peddling furiously up to the house.

Hatti swooped down alongside him, making him swerve, nearly losing his balance. He recovered himself just in time.

'Oh, it's young Hatti. You gave me quite a shock, I thought it might be one of your aunts – no offence meant.'

'Oh, none taken,' said Hatti.

'Would you be a pal, dear Hatti, and bring this letter to your Aunt Grimly.'

'Of course,' said Hatti, taking the letter.

The postman quickly turned his bike around and hurried away.

'Oh, how annoying,' said Abbiewail, as she looked out her bedroom window and watched the postman heading back down the avenue.

Hatti sneaked in the hall door, dropped the letter on the floor and crept up to her room. She was so tired she didn't even wash her teeth. She crawled into her bed, gave a big yawn and settled down to sleep. She was drifting off into a beautiful slumber when a loud shriek startled her awake. Her Aunt Grimly burst into her room.

'Wake up! Wake up! Hatti, I've some important news to tell you.'

'Can't it wait until the morning?' said a very sleepy Hatti.

'It *is* the morning, dear. Come quickly.'

Hatti dragged herself out of bed and crawled down the stairs.

'Oh, tell us,' shrieked Abbiewail. 'The suspense is killing me.'

'What's up?' asked Scarea, as she arrived into the kitchen.

'Sit down, everyone,' said Grimly, waving the letter in the air. She placed her glasses on her nose. 'It's from our dear cousin Whingealot. She's invited us to her 'new' old home in London.'

'Oh no!' said Hatti.

'What!' exclaimed the others.

'I mean, oh yes!' said Hatti quickly. 'That should be very exciting.' Then Hatti added: 'Let's not try and improve London. I'm sure it's lovely just the way it is.'

'There's always room for improvement,' said Abbiewail. 'We mustn't forget to pack our wands, dear sisters.'

'Oh no!' sighed Hatti again.

THE END

Look out for other books in *The Witches' Series*